Sir Lancelot
and the
Ice Castle

Tales of King Arthur

First published in 2006 by
Franklin Watts
338 Euston Road
London
NW1 3BH

Franklin Watts Australia
Hachette Children's Books
Level 17/207 Kent Street
Sydney
NSW 2000

A CIP catalogue record for this book is available
from the British Library.

ISBN (10) 0 7496 6685 4 (hbk)
ISBN (13) 978-0-7496-6685-9 (hbk)
ISBN (10) 0 7496 6698 6 (pbk)
ISBN (13) 978-0-7496-6698-9 (pbk)

Series Editor: Jackie Hamley
Series Advisor: Dr Barrie Wade
Series Designer: Peter Scoulding

Printed in China

Franklin Watts is a division of
Hachette Children's Books.

Sir Lancelot
and the
Ice Castle

by Karen Wallace and Neil Chapman

FRANKLIN WATTS
LONDON•SYDNEY

Sir Lancelot was the bravest knight
at the Round Table. He was loyal
and served King Arthur and
Queen Guinevere well.

King Arthur's sister, Morgana the witch, hated Sir Lancelot. She hated everyone except a knight called Sir Mordred.

Sir Mordred was brave, but he was falling under Morgana's evil spell.

One day, Queen Guinevere rode into the forest. Sir Kay and Sir Mordred went too, but stayed far behind her.

When a stag with white antlers
leapt in front of the Queen,
she chased it through the gates
of a castle made of ice.

Sir Kay and Sir Mordred followed her. They searched everywhere, but all they found were hoof prints around a big white stone!

The knights raced back to tell
King Arthur.

He immediately sent Sir Lancelot
to find the Queen. Sir Kay and
Sir Mordred went with him.

The three knights soon found the Ice Castle. Sir Kay charged through the gates with his sword held high.

When he didn't return,
Sir Lancelot ordered Sir
Mordred to wait outside.

He went into the castle and found
Sir Kay lying frozen on the ground.

Suddenly a huge knight in
white armour appeared.
"I am the White Knight!" he cried.
"I am the Keeper of the Ice Castle!"

"Where is Queen Guinevere?"
demanded Sir Lancelot.
"She will not wake unless you beat
me in battle," said the White Knight.

The White Knight swung his
axe at Sir Lancelot's head.

Sir Lancelot dodged the axe
and hit him with his sword.

In return, the White Knight struck Sir Lancelot's shoulder. "Now your blood will turn to ice," cried the White Knight.

Straight away, Sir Lancelot felt a cold pain spread though his body. But he was determined to save Queen Guinevere before he died.

With a great blow from his sword,
Sir Lancelot split his enemy's
helmet in two.

In front of his eyes, the White
Knight fell apart in a swirl
of snowflakes!

Sir Lancelot saw Queen Guinevere appear. She was lying beside Sir Kay and they were both asleep.

Sir Lancelot felt his own eyes close
and he lay down next to them.

Morgana came inside with
Sir Mordred. She dropped a magic
potion on the lips of Sir Lancelot
and Queen Guinevere.

"Now they will fall in love and want to be together forever," cried Morgana. "King Arthur's kingdom will be destroyed."

Morgana vanished, but her nasty laughter echoed around the Ice Castle. Queen Guinevere and Sir Lancelot woke up and looked at each other.

Morgana's spell came true –
their love began to destroy
the kingdom of Camelot.

Hopscotch has been specially designed to fit the requirements of the National Literacy Strategy. It offers real books by top authors and illustrators for children developing their reading skills. There are 37 Hopscotch stories to choose from:

Marvin, the Blue Pig
ISBN 0 7496 4619 5

Plip and Plop
ISBN 0 7496 4620 9

The Queen's Dragon
ISBN 0 7496 4618 7

Flora McQuack
ISBN 0 7496 4621 7

Willie the Whale
ISBN 0 7496 4623 3

Naughty Nancy
ISBN 0 7496 4622 5

Run!
ISBN 0 7496 4705 1

The Playground Snake
ISBN 0 7496 4706 X

"Sausages!"
ISBN 0 7496 4707 8

The Truth about Hansel and Gretel
ISBN 0 7496 4708 6

Pippin's Big Jump
ISBN 0 7496 4710 8

Whose Birthday Is It?
ISBN 0 7496 4709 4

The Princess and the Frog
ISBN 0 7496 5129 6

Flynn Flies High
ISBN 0 7496 5130 X

Clever Cat
ISBN 0 7496 5131 8

Moo!
ISBN 0 7496 5332 9

Izzie's Idea
ISBN 0 7496 5334 5

Roly-poly Rice Ball
ISBN 0 7496 5333 7

I Can't Stand It!
ISBN 0 7496 5765 0

Cockerel's Big Egg
ISBN 0 7496 5767 7

How to Teach a Dragon Manners
ISBN 0 7496 5873 8

The Truth about those Billy Goats
ISBN 0 7496 5766 9

Marlowe's Mum and the Tree House
ISBN 0 7496 5874 6

Bear in Town
ISBN 0 7496 5875 4

The Best Den Ever
ISBN 0 7496 5876 2

ADVENTURE STORIES

Aladdin and the Lamp
ISBN 0 7496 6678 1 *
ISBN 0 7496 6692 7

Blackbeard the Pirate
ISBN 0 7496 6676 5 *
ISBN 0 7496 6690 0

George and the Dragon
ISBN 0 7496 6677 3 *
ISBN 0 7496 6691 9

Jack the Giant-Killer
ISBN 0 7496 6680 3 *
ISBN 0 7496 6693 5

TALES OF KING ARTHUR

1. The Sword in the Stone
ISBN 0 7496 6681 1 *
ISBN 0 7496 6694 3

2. Arthur the King
ISBN 0 7496 6683 8 *
ISBN 0 7496 6695 1

3. The Round Table
ISBN 0 7496 6684 6 *
ISBN 0 7496 6697 8

4. Sir Lancelot and the Ice Castle
ISBN 0 7496 6685 4 *
ISBN 0 7496 6698 6

TALES OF ROBIN HOOD

Robin and the Knight
ISBN 0 7496 6686 2 *
ISBN 0 7496 6699 4

Robin and the Monk
ISBN 0 7496 6687 0 *
ISBN 0 7496 6700 1

Robin and the Friar
ISBN 0 7496 6688 9 *
ISBN 0 7496 6702 8

Robin and the Silver Arrow
ISBN 0 7496 6689 7 *
ISBN 0 7496 6703 6

* **hardback**